'Good-day, cousin,' said the weasel. 'You smell of a successful hunt.'

'I have killed a rat,' said the stoat. 'I heard you hunting a mouse.'

'There is not much in a mouse,' said the weasel sniffing the rat smell longingly, but knowing very well that he could not share the rat with the stoat. 'Times are bad, cousin.'

Other Enid Blyton Titles published by Red Fox
(incorporating Beaver Books):

MORE
HEDGEROW
TALES

by

Enid Blyton

Illustrated by
Sarah Silcock

RED FOX

A Red Fox Book

Published by Random Century Children's Books
20 Vauxhall Bridge Road, London SW1V 2SA
A division of the Random Century Group

London Melbourne Sydney Auckland
Johannesburg and agencies throughout the world

These stories were first published in *Hedgerow Tales* by
Methuen Children's Books in 1935

Red Fox edition 1991
Text © Darrell Waters Ltd 1935

Set in Plantin
by JH Graphics Ltd, Reading

Printed and bound in Great Britain by
Cox & Wyman Ltd, Reading

ISBN 0 09 980880 3

Contents

Dozymouse and Flittermouse

The little dormouse knew the hedgerow from end to end. He had lived there for two summers and winters, and he knew every creature that ran beneath the hedge, perched in the bushes, or flew in the air above. His big black eyes watched everything.

He was a small, tawny-coloured mouse, with a long thickly-furred tail. He could run and he could climb, and even the oak tree knew him well, for he had many times run up the trunk and along the branches to talk to the squirrel there.

At first the squirrel had thought the dormouse was a tiny squirrel, for he had such a furry tail, such large bright eyes, and the squirrel-like habit of sitting upright with a nut in his paws.

'A squirrel!' said the dormouse in surprise. 'No, not I! I'm one of the mouse family. I've lots of names – dormouse is my right name, but I'm often called Sleepymouse and sometimes Dozy-mouse. I sleep very soundly, you know.'

'Well, I know a queer creature called Flitter-mouse,' said the squirrel. 'You must be a cousin of his.'

'I've never heard of him,' said the dormouse. 'Where does he live?'

'He lives inside the oak tree,' said the squirrel. 'Come and peep.'

The dormouse looked into the hollow trunk of the old oak-tree. He saw something black there, hanging upside down, perfectly still.

'Why,' he said, 'it's a bat! I thought you said it was a flittermouse.'

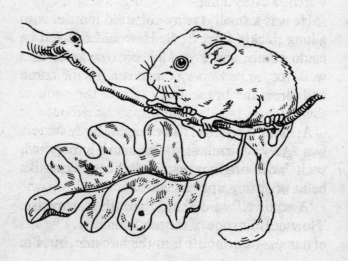

'Well, so it is, isn't it?' said the squirrel. 'It's like a little brown mouse with big black wings that flit about in the dusk – a flittermouse.'

The dormouse woke up the bat. It stretched itself and unfolded its webby wings. It had hung itself up by its hook-like thumbs.

'Is it night-time?' asked the bat in a thin, squeaky voice. 'Are there many flies and beetles about?'

'It is getting dark,' answered the dormouse. 'But, please tell me something. The squirrel says you must be a cousin of mine. But how can you be a mouse if you have wings? You must be a bird.'

'No, no,' said the bat, flying out of the tree and perching very awkwardly beside the dormouse. 'I am no bird. Look at me. I haven't a feather on my back. I don't lay eggs, either.'

'What are your wings made of, then?' asked the dormouse.

'Look!' said the bat, and he stretched out one of his strange wings. 'The bones of my fingers have grown enormously long, and I have grown black skin over my arm and finger bones to make wings. Isn't it a good idea?'

'I wish *I* could do that,' said the dormouse. 'How do you grow yours so long?'

But the bat was off into the air, darting here

and there easily and swiftly. He caught the evening beetles and popped each one into a little pouch he had by his tail. Then he feasted on them, giving high little squeaks of delight as he flew. His eyes were small, and he could not see very well, but his web-like wings were so fine and delicate that he knew at once when he came near trees or bushes.

The dormouse watched him in envy. He liked flies when he could catch them, though he found it better to feed on nuts or grain, for fly-food darted away, and nuts and grain kept still. He peeped inside the oak-tree where the bat had hidden. It smelt strongly of bat.

'I'm glad I don't smell like that,' he said to himself, as he ran quickly down the tree. He stopped at the bottom, and sniffed in every direction. He was always on the look-out for weasels, who loved a feast of dormouse.

There was no enemy near, so the dormouse ran to his summer nest to tell his wife to come out and hunt. He went to the hedgerow and clambered up the brambles. A little way up was his nest, in which he had had several families of tiny dormice that summer. Now the last of them had gone, and all were running about on their own. The dormouse sometimes met them in the hedgerow, but most of them had grown so big that he hardly knew them.

The nest was well made, tucked into the bramblestems. The dormouse had decided to make it of the bark from the stems of the old honeysuckle that grew farther down the hedgerow. He had torn it off in long strips, and he and his wife had made their nest with leaves, so that it was cosy and warm. It was so well hidden that not even the rabbit guessed where it was.

In the daytime the dormice hid in their nest and slept soundly. At night they woke up and went hunting for food. They loved nuts, berries and grain, and if they chanced upon a fat caterpillar they would take that too. As the summer went by they grew fatter and fatter, and their nest shook with their weight!

'When the autumn comes we must build a nest underground,' said the dormice. 'This one will be too easily seen when the bramble-leaves fall.'

When October came the dormice were so fat and round that there really was not enough room for them both in their nest. The nights became chilly. The dormice felt more and more sleepy.

So they hunted about and at last found a little

tunnel going right down among the roots of the hedgerow, quite a long way underground. They took some moss down the hole and arranged it in a little round place among the roots. They would be warm and comfortable there, far away from any enemy.

'Now we must take plenty of food down to our new nest,' said the dormouse to his wife. 'We might wake up on a warm winter's day and feel hungry.'

It was while they were hunting for food that they heard the bat calling to them. The dormouse once again climbed the oak tree and looked at the queer little bat clinging clumsily to a branch.

'I want to say goodbye,' said the bat. 'It's getting cold now, and I am going to hide myself away for the winter.'

'We are just doing the same!' said the dormouse in surprise. 'We have made a nice nest far underground among the hedgerow roots, and we are hoarding up some food in case we wake up on a warm winter's day and want a meal.'

'I don't do that,' said the bat. 'My food wouldn't keep like yours. It would go bad, because it is beetles and flies. If I wake up it will be such a warm spell that a few flies are sure to be about, too, and I shall catch them. I am going to fly to an old cave I know across the fields. A

great many of my relations will be there, big bats and little bats, long-eared bats and short-eared ones, and little common bats like myself.'

'Do you make a nest?' asked the dormouse.

'Of course not!' said the bat. 'No bat ever makes a nest! We shall all hang ourselves up by our hooked thumbs upside down, cover ourselves with our wings and go fast asleep.'

'What do you do with your young ones if you don't make a nest to keep them in?' asked the dormouse in surprise.

'Oh, we keep our little ones cuddled against our fur, even when we fly in the air,' answered

13

the bat. 'They cling tightly and never fall. Well, dormouse, I hope I see you well and fat in the springtime. You look fat enough now!'

'So do you!' said the little dormouse.

'Ah, it's a good thing to get fat before the long, hungry winter-time!' said the bat. 'We shall get through the cold days comfortably then. Well, goodbye.'

'Just come and see my nest before you go,' begged the dormouse.

'I can't,' said the bat, impatiently. 'Haven't you seen my knees? They turn backwards instead of forwards, so that I can't walk. I am only made for flying!'

He rose into the air and darted swiftly away. 'Goodbye, little flittermouse!' called the dormouse, and then, feeling a touch of frost in the air, he ran quickly to his hole. His small fat wife was waiting for him. Without a word they curled up together in the warm moss and fell asleep. They became as cold as ice, they seemed not to breathe, so soundly asleep were they – but a warm night would awaken them, and then they would feast eagerly on their little store of nuts in the roots of the hedgerow.

The Spinner in
the Hedge

It was a warm and sunny November day. After a few cold nights, which had sent hundreds of leaves fluttering from the hedgerow into the ditch below, there had come a warm spell. Today the sky was blue, and only a few wispy clouds were to be seen.

The hedgerow gleamed yellow, pink and red. It still had some leaves left on it – bright crimson blackberry sprays that waved high in the air, a few golden hazel leaves and some red and yellow hawthorn leaves. The ivy was green and thick. It did not drop its leaves in the autumn, but shed a few all year round. There were still flies buzzing about the late blossoms, and a big queen wasp tempted out by the sunshine. It was warm in the shelter of the hedge – so warm that a little colony of sparrows, on their way back from the hayricks, had stopped to preen their feathers there.

15

A big spider was watching the birds carefully. It was an old and wise spider. It knew the unexpected ways of toads, who could shoot out a tongue and snap up fly or spider in a twink. It had seen the cleverness of the swallows that could catch any insect that flew.

The spider was not very much afraid of the sparrows. She had often watched their clumsiness when they tried to catch an insect on the wing. She knew she could dart away and hide if one of the little brown birds saw her. What she was worrying about was her web. She had made a very fine web the night before, for she had guessed that the day would be warm and that there might be flies about. She was hungry and wanted a good meal.

Now the sparrows were sitting in a heap near the web. If one of them fluttered his wings, the web would break and all the spider's work would be wasted. And then, even as she watched, it happened. Two sparrows began to fight, and one of them fell. Straight through the fine, silky web he tumbled, and the spider, angry and frightened, ran through the hedgerow to get away from the noise and the scuffling.

Suddenly the sparrows spread their wings and flew away – all but one. He decided to stay where he was. It was warm and sunny in the hedge, he was very full of seeds, and he didn't want to move. He flew to the top of a blackberry spray and perched there in the sunshine.

The spider was just about to climb up the very same spray. She had made up her mind to make a new web there, stretched from that spray to another near by. She had noticed that a great many flies seemed to fly over the hedgerow just there.

She made an angry noise when the small sparrow perched, swinging, on her spray. The sparrow heard it and saw her.

'What's the matter?' he asked in surprise. 'Why do you glare at me like that with all your eight eyes? Don't be afraid of me – I shan't eat you today. I've just had a fine feast of seeds from the hayrick.'

'You have perched on the spray I wanted for my web,' said the spider, glowering. 'Can't you move?'

'Yes, if you'll let me see you making your web,' said the sparrow, who was still young enough to like watching things. He hopped to another spray.

The spider took a good look at the young sparrow, and as he really did seem very small and very fat, she thought it would be safe to get on with her web. So she began.

'It's easy,' she said. 'Any spider knows how to spin. I have little knobs underneath me, my spinnerets, and from them comes the thread for my webs. I can make it sticky or not, as I like.

The sparrow watched the spider make four threads, two at the bottom and two at the sides of the blackberry sprays. Then he watched her go to the middle of the top thread and drop down to the middle of the bottom thread, leaving a new thread behind her. She climbed half-way up this thread, and then began to travel up and down from the middle thread to the outside threads, making the spokes of her web as she went.

18

When all the spokes were finished the spider went back to the middle again, and began to make the spiral thread that wound round and round and round the spokes until she reached the outside threads. Then back went the spider to the middle again, weaving another spiral thread, but as she went, she ate up the first spiral!

The sparrow was astonished. What a waste of work! Then he noticed that the second spiral was hung with sticky drops.

'Why do you put those drops there?' he asked. 'They look sticky.'

'Of course they are sticky!' said the spider, scornfully. 'When a fly comes by, it flies into the web and gets caught on the stickiness.'

'But why don't *you* get caught in your own web?' asked the sparrow, surprised.

'Because I am sensible enough to keep my legs well oiled,' answered the spider. 'If I didn't oil them well, I *should* stick to my own web. Look at the ends of my feet – do you see my comb-like claws? I can hold easily to the thin threads of my web with those claws. Now I am going to hide under this leaf and see if I can catch a fly in my web. There is nothing more for you to see, so you can go. I don't want you to break my web with your clumsy feet.'

But the young sparrow didn't go. He stayed there, watching. Soon a small fly came hurrying by, anxious to get to the ivy blossom it could smell. It didn't see the web and flew straight into it. The spider felt the web shaking, and rushed down from her leaf. In a trice she plunged her jaws into the struggling fly and paralysed it. She sucked its blood. Back she went to her hiding place and waited patiently.

Almost at once a big bluebottle buzzed by. He saw the sparrow and turned back in fear, only to catch his wings in the web. At once the waiting spider hurried down again – but when she saw the big fly she paused.

Then she quickly made up her mind what to do. She ran to where he was struggling and began to cut the web here and there. At last she had cut all the threads but one that held the fly. She began to twirl the wretched insect round and round on the one thread, and as she spun him round she let out another thread that bound him more and more closely as he twirled helplessly round. Then when he was quite harmless she ran down to him and killed him.

That was a fine feast for her. The watching sparrow began to feel quite afraid of the clever spinner. He was glad he was too big for her to weave a web around *him*. Then there came a

loud droning sound and a queen wasp sailed by.
She flew right into the middle of the web, and
in her struggles she became wrapped round and
round with it.

'Let me out,' she buzzed, angrily. 'Let me
out. If you don't let me out I shall sting you to
death.'

The spider ran in alarm to her leaf and hid
there. But the big queen wasp buzzed even more
loudly.

'You are a hateful creature to weave snares for
us insects. Insects should help one another.'

'You are an insect, but I am not,' said the

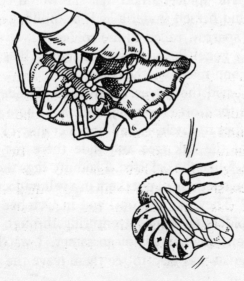

spider, peering out. 'You have six legs and I have eight. And why do you talk about insects helping one another? I have seen you pounce on flies and nip off their wings before taking them to your grubs. I shall not let you go.'

'Then I will destroy your web,' said the wasp, fiercely. 'I will get away from it and then I will sting you to death.'

She struggled so fiercely that the spider was frightened. She ran out and began to cut the threads that bound the wasp. When she had cut them all, the wasp dropped down into the hedgerow. She began to clean the web from her body. The spider, afraid that she would come back, hid herself under a leaf, trembling.

The sparrow called to the spider

'She's gone! But your web is spoilt,' he said. 'Come and make another one.'

'No,' said the spider. 'I am tired. Besides, I believe the frost is coming, and then there will be no flies to catch. I shall find a cranny in the bark of the oak tree and hide there for the winter. I like the oak tree. I laid my eggs there. Did you see them? I put them in a yellow cocoon of silk. They hatched out, and in October the tiny spiders all went adventuring through the fields on long threads of gossamer. I watched them go. I was glad to see them leave the oak tree, because I did not want them to stay and catch my flies.'

'Yes, I saw the young spiders,' said the sparrow, spreading his wings to fly. 'I ate some. Perhaps one day I shall come back and eat *you* so be careful!'

He flew away. The spider ran up the trunk of the oak tree, and very soon hid herself under a rough piece of bark. She huddled there, looking shrivelled and dead – but she was only pretending! She could come alive in a twinkling if she wanted to!

The Grey Miner

The hedgerow stood bare and cold in the winter sunshine. The frost had stripped the last few leaves from the hawthorn, hazel and brambles, and only the ivy was green. The oak tree that spread its big branches overhead still had some rustling brown leaves left, and those shone like old copper in the sunshine.

The leaves from the hedgerow lay in dry heaps in the ditch below. They crackled when any creature trod on them. Their bright colours had faded to a dull brown; the little creatures of the hedgerow found them useful for nest-linings, for the dry leaves were cosy and warm to sleep in.

There were not many hedgerow folk about now. It was too cold. The dormice were fast asleep. The lizards and newts were hidden safely away, and the bat had hung himself upside down in a nearby cave. It was winter-time.

There was one little creature very busy on this

sunshiny November day. He did not go to sleep for the winter as some of the hedgerow creatures did, because he was always too hungry to sleep for long. He was a little grey mole, the miner of the hedgerow.

He lived so much underground that his eyes were almost no use to him, they had become so deeply buried in his velvety fur. But he had little use for eyes – it was his nose and his ears that helped him to find his food!

All through the summer days he had hunted for worms, grubs, slugs and beetles. He had gone down the underground runs that had been used by hundreds of moles before – long, straight runs worn smooth and round by the passing of many velvety bodies. From these runs the mole had tunnelled sideways in search of worms, throwing up the earth as he went, making many little molehills that showed the way he had gone.

Now that the winter had come there were fewer creatures about, and sometimes many days passed before the mole met anyone on his journeys, except little grey miners like himself. Today he was frightened, for a strange thing had happened. He had had a nest deep in a molehill on the other side of the field, not far from a little brook. For four days the rain had fallen without

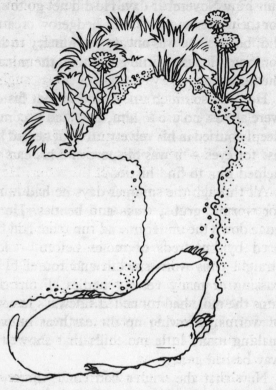

stopping, and at the end of the fourth day the brook had overflowed its banks. The water had flooded the mole's main tunnel and had poured into his nest.

In a great fright, the little creature began to tunnel upwards, and at last came up into the open air on the very top of his molehill. Water was all around him – only the height of his hill saved him from the flood.

Soon the water went down a little, and the mole stepped into it. He did not dare to tunnel downwards, for he was afraid of being caught by the water below ground. He found that the water round his hill was deep, but he could swim well; so away he went, striking out with his spade-like front paws as fast as he could.

Soon he came to the end of the water. He was on the earth again. He burrowed downwards, throwing out the mould with his paws, and at last struck a tunnel, one of the many that ran across the field. He went along it and reached the hedgerow, which he knew quite well. There was a fine straight run that ran all along the hedgerow. It was dry and felt warm. The mole made up his mind to make a new nest under the hedge there. He began to make a side tunnel towards the hedgerow.

His sharp nose smelt a worm as he worked. At once he thrust his strong snout into the earth and dug swiftly with his clawed feet. In a trice he reached the worm, which lay coiled up cosily in its small chamber of earth, and he gobbled it up greedily. Then he went on with his tunnelling.

Now just nearby was a fine hole used by a

hedgehog for her winter sleep. She lay curled up there, dry and warm. When the back wall of her hole gave way and the mole appeared behind her, the hedgehog woke up in a fright. She at once thought it was an enemy, and she curled herself up all the more tightly.

'Move yourself,' said the mole, pushing up against the frightened hedgehog. He had a high, squeaky voice like a bat. 'I am tunnelling here.'

The hedgehog knew the mole's voice, and uncurled at once.

'Why do you disturb me?' she asked, angrily. 'I was fast asleep. You should sleep, too, in this cold weather.'

'I wish I could,' said the mole. 'But I am always too hungry. Do you know whether there are many grubs about under this hedgerow? I should like to find some of those fat grey leather-jackets; they make a fine meal, and I am very hungry.'

The hedgehog looked at the mole's velvety coat, so different from her own mass of spines.

'You will find plenty of worms and grubs in this bank,' she said. 'Tell me, how do you manage to keep your coat so clean and tidy, living underground as you do, tunnelling all day long?'

'It's easy,' said the mole. 'My coat is very short and all the hairs stand straight up – they do not lie backwards like the rabbit's. So it doesn't really matter if I go forwards or backwards in my tunnels – the hairs will bend either way quite easily. Why don't you tunnel, too? You have a long snout, like mine, and could easily burrow with it.'

'No, I couldn't,' said the hedgehog. 'I use it for turning over leaves when I look for slugs, but it isn't strong like yours. I have seen you thrusting your snout into the earth and throwing it up easily. May I see your paws? I have often wanted to see how it is you can dig so well.'

The mole held out a front hand. It was very curious, for the palm was turned outwards, instead of inwards. It was very broad, and the nails were large and strong. The mole could not close his hand; he always had to hold it open. It was immensely strong, exactly the right shape for digging and tunnelling.

'I shall have my nest under this hedgerow,' said the mole. 'It seems a good place. I can smell plenty of worms about.'

'How do you build your nest?' asked the hedgehog, sleepily. 'I just find a hole and line it with leaves and moss.'

'Oh, I shall tunnel until I am right under the hedge,' said the mole. 'Then I shall make a nice hole there, throwing up the earth above it till there is quite a big hill above my hole. I expect I shall have to make one or two tunnels from my hole through the hill above to throw out all the earth. If I feel cold I shall line my hole with a few leaves, as you have done. The hole will be my resting place, but when I am not there I shall be hunting all around under the ground for grubs and worms.'

'Don't eat them all,' begged the hedgehog. 'I might go hunting myself on a warm winter's night.'

'Tell me when you do, and I'll take you to the best hunting-ground,' promised the mole.

'Will you have any children living with you in your nest?' asked the hedgehog, remembering how she had had seven little hedgehogs with her in the summer-time.

'Oh no,' said the mole. 'I never have them in *my* nest. I had a wife who made a very big nest for our young ones this summer. It was out in the middle of the field, though I warned her it was not a good place. She took leaves and grasses to her hole in her mouth, to make the nest nice and soft. I saw the young moles. They were queer, wrinkled little creatures. But before they could look after themselves a dog came and smelt them out. He destroyed the nest-hill and found the little ones. My wife escaped down the tunnel, but she was so frightened that she fled to another field.'

'A badger ate one of *my* little ones,' said the hedgehog, suddenly remembering the pitiful squeak she had heard when the tiny creature had been caught. 'All the rest are grown up and have found holes of their own to sleep in. I don't think I should know them now if I met them again. You had better go now, mole. I want to sleep again.'

The hedgehog curled herself up tightly and in a few minutes was snoring softly. The mole turned and went back into his tunnel. He dug hard for a few minutes, ate three worms and a grub, and then found himself just underneath the thickest part of the hedgerow, where he planned to make his nest.

He began to loosen the earth with his strong, spade-like paws. He pushed it upwards with his snout. As the hole became big, so the hill above grew big, too, for all the earth from the hole was thrown there. Soon the mole had to take the earth right up through the hill, and to do that he had to tunnel up it. But it was not long before he had the inner hole big enough to satisfy himself. He settled down in it comfortably to have a short sleep, for he was tired. His hill rose up under the brambles in the hedgerow and was well hidden.

He fell asleep and dreamed of all the things he liked so much to eat. The rabbits came out of their hole and looked at the new mound of earth in the hedgerow.

'A mole has come to live here,' they said. 'We shall sometimes meet him where his tunnels cross our burrows. Our hedgerow will shelter yet one more creature this winter!'

The oak tree rustled loudly. It would feel yet another patter of feet over its deep and tangled roots, and it was glad.

Keep Away!

From the time when the hedgerow had first been planted until now, when it had grown high and thick, the birds had lived here. They had nested there, hunted for food among the leaves, roosted there at night, and sung from the topmost sprays when their young ones had hatched out. The hedgerow had heard many different songs and calls, and had hidden many a neatly made nest.

The little brown wren was always flitting in and out of the hedge; the quiet hedge-sparrow had for two years built her nest there, and laid inside it her pretty, sky-blue eggs; the chaffinch had once built a beautiful nest in the ivy leaves, and had trimmed it outside with lichen from the ditch beneath. But the bird that the hedgerow knew best of all was the robin redbreast.

The robin was such an inquisitive, restless little bird. Whatever happened in or under the hedgerow he had to know about. If a hedgehog came shuffling by, the robin flitted about above him in the hedge. If a weasel glided silently along in the ditch below, the robin set up a loud tick-tick-tick sound and warned every other creature in the hedgerow so that they fled for shelter. He was always about, from dawn to dusk, and was the last to go to roost.

In the springtime two or three robins were to be seen in the hedgerow, but when winter came only one sang his creamy little song there. He lived there, and rarely left the hedge and the surrounding piece of meadow. He hunted for worms in the grass, and rooted about for insects in the moist ditch. There were not very many for him to find, so he became rather thin – but he didn't *look* thin, because the cold weather made him fluff out his feathers and look twice as big as he really was!

One day another robin flew down to the hedgerow and looked around. He was a handsome fellow, bold and lively. His bright black eyes flashed, and he flicked his wings and bobbed his tail up and down. Then he gave a rich little trill.

The other robin, who had lived in the hedge all the autumn and part of the winter, heard the song at once and answered it defiantly.

'How dare you come to my hedge?' he sang.

'This is my piece of ground. Keep away! Keep away!'

'It is a nice hedge!' sang back the second robin. 'I will have it for my own.'

Two bullfinches poked their heads out from the ivy, where they had been sitting side by side. They felt sure there was going to be a fight. That would make the fifth fight this winter between robins.

'Quarrelsome creatures!' said the cock bullfinch, fluffing out his brick-red chest. 'Why can't they live in peace with one another, as you and I do all the year round, little wife?'

The two robins were now shouting their warsong so loudly that a horde of inquisitive sparrows flew up to see what was the matter. 'Cheer up, cheer up, cheer up!' they cried, excitedly.

'This is my hedge, I tell you!' sang the first robin. 'Keep away from it, or I will fight you!'

'Then fight me, for I say it is *my* hedge!' sang the second robin. With that the two small birds flung themselves at one another, still singing loudly, and began to fight. How they pecked! How they struck with their quivering wings! And how they sang! It was marvellous to hear. The sparrows were immensely excited, and cheered loudly. Only the two bullfinches were disgusted.

The hen bullfinch peered out again and gave a little cry of horror.

'Will you believe it! The second robin is the hedgerow robin's *son*! Yes, he is. I know him by a tiny white feather in one wing. To think that a robin should fight his father, and a father his son!'

The bullfinches chattered together, and rubbed their cone-shaped beaks lovingly one against the other. They were affectionate birds, and had lived together for five years, building a nest each year and helping one another always.

They remembered quite well how happy the robin had been that spring when he and his lively little wife had come hunting for a nesting place in the hedgerow. The cock bird had wanted to nest low down in the hedge, and they had almost decided on a place when the hen robin gave a wild trill of joy.

'Look! Here is an old boot thrown in the ditch!' she sang. 'Let us build there! I love to build my nest in something that humans have used. Last year my nest was in an old kettle, and the year before I built it in a tin.'

'I was brought up in an old saucepan,' said her mate. 'Last year I had a wife and we built our nest in a watering can in the garden of a house. I like humans. They are kind and friendly. They throw out crumbs for us, and when they work in their gardens they dig up grubs for us to eat. They are nice creatures. I would love dearly to build our nest in something they have used. Let us look at the old boot.'

So they hopped down to the ditch and examined the dirty, gaping old boot. It was just what they wanted. How pleased they were! How they sang about it! The two bullfinches, who had just decided to build their nest in the hedge above, thought that the two robins were mad to choose such a queer place when they could have chosen a nice, cosy home in the hedge.

The robins made a big, bulky nest inside the

boot. They used the old brown oak-leaves in the
ditch, and some soft moss. They lined the nest
with cow hairs and three chicken feathers they
had found at the farm across the fields. Then the
hen laid four pretty eggs mottled with light red,
and the two birds were as happy as the day was
long.

The bullfinches had been happy, too. Their
nest was quite different. It was a frail little plat-
form of sticks, very cunningly woven. On it the
bullfinches had placed a cup-like arrangement
of roots, and inside they had neatly lined it with
sheep hairs and cow hairs. The hen had laid five
beautiful eggs, a dark green-blue, streaked with
purple and red. The young robins and
bullfinches had hatched out at exactly the same

time, and the hen birds had been most interested in each other's nestlings. They had often gone to peep into one another's nest.

The cock robin was so proud of his brood of nestlings that he had sung about them loudly whenever he had a moment to spare, which was not often, for they were very hungry little creatures. The hen loved them, too, and when the weasel had come slipping by she had been almost mad with fear. But all the nestlings had been reared safely, and the robins had had a second family in the old boot.

Then the bullfinches had seen a most extraordinary thing. When autumn came the little hen had wanted to live in the hedgerow, but the cock robin had driven her angrily away. The two bullfinches had watched in horror. They lived joyfully together all the year round, and they could not understand such ways. Now here was the cock robin fighting again – this time with his own son.

'I shall go and stop them,' said the cock bullfinch at last. 'They are making such a noise that the sparrowhawk will hear and come swooping down on us.'

He flew to where the two robins were fighting. Just as he got there the old robin gave the young one such a vicious peck that he fell to the ground. As soon as he touched the grass he was up again, and he flew over the hedge and away to the wood as fast as ever he could, quite defeated.

'Keep away, keep away!' trilled the old robin. 'This is *my* hedgerow.'

'You should be ashamed to fight your own family,' said the bullfinch. 'I never fight *my* family.'

'Oh, you!' said the robin, scornfully. 'You don't need to! You can feed on all kinds of things easy to find in the wintertime – seeds, berries, winter buds. But we robins are different. We feed on insects, and they are very difficult to get in the wintertime. One hedgerow, bank and ditch will only feed one robin – so we each have our own beat in winter and must keep to it. That son of mine I fought just now ought to know better than to come here! This hedgerow is mine! I tell you, all robins must have their own little piece of ground in the winter or starve! It is a wise rule. This is my hedgerow, I say!'

The bullfinch flew off. He thought there was something in what the robin said – or rather sang, for all of his long speech had been trilled at the top of his liquid voice. After all, insects *were* very scarce in the winter. If three or four robins all lived in the same place they would certainly starve to death.

'What did he say to you?' asked the hen bullfinch.

'He told me why he fought,' said the bullfinch. 'I think he is right, after all. Robins must fight in the winter, but bullfinches need not. Shall we go and find some dock seeds?'

They flew off – and as they went they heard the robin singing at the top of his lovely voice. 'Keep away! Keep away! This is my hedgerow! Keep away!'

Never Say Die!

All day long and all night long, too, there was a coming and going in the hedgerow. Rabbits and voles, mice and rats, birds of all kinds went to and fro about their business, squeaking, chirping, chattering. Usually the hedgerow folk were happy and contented, but sometimes there came a great outcry and disturbance when a hated enemy came slinking by or flew from overhead.

'Stoat!' would come the signal from a wary rabbit, and at once all the hedgerow folk would vanish. 'Sparrowhawk!' was another cry, feared by the many chirruping sparrows. 'Owl!' would squeak a terrified mouse at night, peeping from his hole to see a shadowy wing passing overhead.

The blackbird was a good friend to all the little creatures in the hedgerow. He often sat high up on the oak tree to sing his beautiful, flute-like song, and from his high branch he could see many things. He could see the brown, slinking stoat, and he could spy the smaller weasel, gliding like a snake along the ditch.

Then he would give the alarm, and his loud, harsh cries would go ringing up the hedgerow and down, striking fear into every small, beating heart. Mice, rabbits, voles, birds – they would all take flight, silently and fearfully.

The cunning stoat or sly weasel would stay still by a tuft of grass, hating the blackbird, whose sharp eyes had seen him gliding along. But the blackbird, safe in the tree, cared nothing, and as long as he saw the enemy below he continued to send out his alarm call, warning all the furred and feathered folk to keep under cover.

But for a long time no weasel or stoat had come to the hedgerow, and life had been peaceful. The owl had come two or three times at night, and the sparrowhawk had flashed round the hedge after a frightened chaffinch one late afternoon – but there had been nothing very frightening besides these two happenings.

For the last two or three weeks something strange had come to the hedgerow – something that puzzled the little folk very much. Soft white flakes had fallen from the sky, and the fields all around were covered with a white blanket, cold and soft to tiny paws. The weather had turned cold again, and the snow had come to pile up in drifts here and there, and to cover every tree and bush with white.

The mice made narrow runs under the snow. The rabbits came out and tried to find grass beneath it, but they were half-scared at the strange, white glare of the fields. Some of them went to nibble at the bark of the ivy, for they were very hungry. The rats grew thin and fierce, and grumbled bitterly among themselves.

'We cannot get near that store of mangolds,' said one. 'There is a weasel there, and he kills every rat that ventures near.'

'The mice are difficult to catch in this snow,' said another rat, showing his sharp teeth. 'They would be good to eat, for they are fat with feasting on their stores of hidden seeds.'

The rats were crouching in the snowy ditch, sniffing at a pile of dry little bones, which had once belonged to a thrush, killed in the autumn. Only the bones were left now, and the rats knew there was no joy to be had from eating them. One of the rats was weak with hunger, and a fierce-looking companion was eyeing it, wondering if he could fight it and kill it. Just as he was about to spring on his companion, a whisper went through the hedgerow.

'Stoat! Stoat!'

The rats scattered and vanished – all but the
one who had been about to spring on his weak
companion. The stoat had come swiftly behind
him and sprung swiftly. The rat lay on his side,
bitten deeply in the neck. He was dead.

The stoat looked round him and sniffed. He
was in the ditch, and the snow there was much
trodden by little feet. He could smell mice, too,

45

and the little pile of thrush bones. And he could smell rabbit.

Rabbit! The stoat was lean and hungry, for hunting had been bad. He longed for a meal of rabbit – but, meanwhile, here was the dead rat, and that was good for a starving stoat.

He could hardly be seen against the snow, for he was pure white all over, save for a black tip to his tail. His eyes were dark and fierce, and stared steadily around him as he feasted on the rat. Suddenly he pricked up his ears. He could hear sounds on the other side of the hedge – a frightened squeak and a flurry of snow. The stoat shot up the side of the ditch and leapt up the bank. He saw a hole in the hedge and ran to it.

At the very same moment a brown creature arrived at the hole from the other side, and the two met, nose to nose. They backed a little and glared at one another. Then they recognized each other, and flashed a greeting from their bright black eyes.

'Good day, cousin,' said the weasel. 'You smell of a successful hunt.'

'I have killed a rat,' said the stoat. 'I heard you hunting a mouse.'

'There is not much in a mouse,' said the weasel, sniffing the rat smell longingly, but knowing very well that he could not share the rat with the stoat. 'Times are bad, cousin.'

'Never say die!' said the stoat, going back to the dead rat. 'That is our motto, cousin! Never say die! We are fierce and strong, and as long as there is an enemy to be hunted we will hunt him.'

'Cousin stoat,' said the weasel, who had been eyeing the stoat's coat in surprise, 'how is it that you are white like the snow now? You were red-brown when I last saw you, and if it had not been for your large, bright eyes and your stoat smell I would not have known you.'

'My coat has turned white since the snow came,' answered the stoat. 'How can I hunt well if my coat is brown when the snow is so white? I should be too easily seen. So my coat has changed, and only the tip of my tail has stayed black. I shall change back again to my usual red-brown coat when the warm weather comes.'

'It is a strange thing, but most useful,' said the weasel. 'You are lucky, cousin. You are larger than I am, to begin with, which makes you a more dangerous enemy, and now that you are white you are most difficult to see! I am glad I am not your enemy!'

'I should like a good meal of young rabbit,'

said the stoat, 'but they do not come out so much now that the snow is here.'

'I have tried my best to catch a rabbit,' said the weasel, 'but I am too easily seen now. My coat shows up so plainly in the snow. Wait, though! I may be able to catch one in another way. There are plenty of rabbits in this hedgerow, I know. I once had a nest here with my wife, and we saw hundreds of rabbits about these fields. When she took our little ones out to teach them hunting they had plenty to eat. Would you like to see me catch a rabbit without chasing it, cousin?'

'Yes,' said the stoat, who was now well fed and quite agreeable to lying down in the snow and watching someone else hunt.

'Then watch me,' said the small weasel, his short tail quivering with excitement and his large black eyes fierce with hunger. He glided down to the ditch and then up the side of it into the field. The stoat watched him.

The weasel sat in the snow for a moment, quite silent. He could see a few rabbits watching him from their holes, ready to bolt at once if he came near. Then he began to do most extraordinary things, quite amazing to watch.

He squirmed from side to side. He threw himself up in the air and down. He leapt sideways, he turned himself round and round and round. He flung himself over and rolled on his back, and then he sprang the right way up and bounded round in a circle. The watching rabbits could hardly believe their eyes. What was happening to this weasel? *Could* it be a weasel if it behaved so queerly? They had never seen anything so strange before.

Three rabbits came right out of their holes to watch more closely. A small mouse looked out from his little burrow. A dozen sparrows sat chattering in the trees, astonished at the sight of the weasel behaving as if he were completely mad. The blackbird flew up, too, and looked to see what was happening. He saw the weasel and was just about to utter his cry of alarm to warn everyone else, when he found that the weasel was rolling over and over on the ground. Was he hurt? Why was he behaving like that? Now look at him, jumping up in the air as if he were mad! The blackbird was amazed, and forgot to utter his alarm cry.

One of the rabbits, a young one, only born the summer before, moved closer to the strange weasel. He was fascinated, puzzled, amazed. The weasel watched him from unblinking black eyes. And then a memory came into the mind of the blackbird on the bough. He had seen this before!

'It's a trick!' cried the blackbird in his ringing voice. 'It's a trick! Beware, you rabbits! Run, mouse! It's a trick, I tell you! He'll catch you! He'll catch you!'

The mouse disappeared. Two of the rabbits bolted. The sparrows flew to the top of the oak tree, chirruping in terror. Only one rabbit remained, and he seemed not to hear what the blackbird said. The weasel heard, and his bright eyes flashed in hate at the blackbird who was spoiling his sport. He ran round and round in a narrow circle, whilst the rabbit sat and watched him, his nose trembling in delight at the astonishing scene.

The weasel widened his circle a little, and the watching stoat, hidden in the ditch, stiffened. He knew quite well that the weasel was going to strike very soon now. All his hairs rose on his back and his tail swelled.

Almost at once the weasel darted at the rabbit, flung himself on the startled creature's neck and gave him the death-bite. The rabbit gave a pitiful squeak and died. The stoat came out from his hiding place and eyed the feast, not daring to join in, for he feared the savage little weasel.

'Never say die!' said the starving weasel in triumph. 'If one trick doesn't serve, another will.'

'I told you so, I told you so!' cried the blackbird to the dead rabbit.

'He was always a foolish little creature,' said the other rabbits, hidden close in their burrow. 'It is a wonder he lived so long. Poor, silly little rabbit!'

Hoo Hoo the Owl

The snow had gone, vanished in a day and a night. The countryside was muddy and wet, and in the warm sunshine the ditches sent up a faint steam. The wind blew warm and soft – spring was coming!

All the folk of the hedgerow felt it and rejoiced. The hedgehog stirred and woke. The grey squirrels left their hiding places and frisked about in the trees, disliking the ground because of the mud that stuck to their paws. The freckled thrush began to look for a nesting place, and so did the robin. The blackbird sang loudly and beautifully in the mornings and evenings. The hedgerow folk were happy and excited, enjoying the warm sunshine and soft winds.

The sparrowhawk was also thinking of nesting. He had a fine mate, bigger than he was, and she wanted a good nest in a safe place.

'I built in an old magpie's nest last year,' she said, 'and it was very comfortable. Let us see if we can find another. It will save a lot of trouble if we find one, and use it for the base of ours. It is easy to build on the top of an old nest.'

So they hunted about, swooping over the tops of hedges together, and frightening all the little birds terribly, for there is no hope for a bird caught by a sparrowhawk. But this time the hawks were not hunting for food, they were looking for a nesting place.

At last they came to the old oak tree that shaded the hedgerow. There were no leaves on it yet, for it was barely March, but by the time the eggs were laid it would be May and the oak would be leafing. There would be plenty of shelter for the sparrowhawks then, when they went to and from the nest.

'See!' cried the cock sparrowhawk, as he spied the hollow in the tree. 'There is an old squirrel's nest here. It must have belonged to the squirrel who was once in this tree. Shall we take it for ours, and build our nest in it?'

The hen sparrowhawk hopped inside and looked carefully all round. 'This will do,' she said, pleased. 'It is just the place. We will not begin yet, because it is early in the year – but we will roost here at night so that all the hedgerow creatures may know this nest is to be ours.'

What consternation, what horror there was in the hedgerow when the sparrows, chaffinches and robins heard what the sparrowhawks were going to do! Hawks right in the midst of the hedgerow! Small birds would be hunted and killed there every day. Mice would disappear. Voles would be caught for the young hawks. The hedgerow was full of talk and rage from end to end. It was the most terrible thing that had ever happened.

The sparrowhawks were as good as their word. They roosted in the squirrel's nest at night, and in the daytime they flew swiftly and silently along the hedgerow, seeking for unwary birds. Then the sparrows were thankful for the thick ivy that made up part of the hedge, for once hidden in its close greenery they were safe.

One day there was a great disturbance in the pine woods on the other side of the field. Blackbirds shouted, starlings chattered, sparrows chirruped furiously. All the small birds in the hedgerow heard the commotion and flew off to see what it was about. They soon found out. It was a tawny owl who had hidden himself

closely in a pine-tree to roost until night. A blackbird had discovered him, and had given the alarm.

'Owl! Owl! Hiding here in this tree! Come and see, come and see!'

And at once every bird within call flew up. How they scolded the owl! How they shouted at him, calling him the rudest names they knew! They hated the owl because he sometimes caught a sparrow, but mostly because they thought his face was like a cat's. Any bird that looked like a cat must be bad, thought the birds.

The owl sat perfectly still, looking at the angry birds out of eyes almost shut. When he could bear the noise no longer he spread his big, soft wings and flew suddenly out of the tree. All the birds followed, flying after him, chattering in their shrillest voices.

'Mob him! Mob him! Chase him away!'

The owl flew over the field and made for the old oak tree. He knew there was a hollow place there, and he thought it would be a good hiding place. He was tired of all these stupid, noisy birds. He flew to a low branch, walked rather clumsily up it and disappeared into the hollow where the squirrel's old nest was. Then he sat perfectly still and waited. To his surprise no birds came to scold him. Everything was silent outside.

No wonder! It was the time of day when the two sparrowhawks liked to pounce swiftly along the hedgerow, and no little bird wished to be there then. So, because of the coming of the sparrowhawks, the owl was left to himself. He was glad. He closed his great round eyes and slept.

The sun sank in a red sky. Darkness crept over the fields. Suddenly there was a scrambling noise outside the hollow, and to the owl's surprise someone came into his hole. It was the cock sparrowhawk, come with his mate to roost for the night.

The owl was disturbed. He hissed angrily. The sparrowhawk stopped in alarm. 'There is a snake here,' he called to his wife. The owl hooted with laughter.

'Hoo hoo hoo!' he cried. 'Hoo hoo hoo-hoo-oooooooooo!'

'It's an owl!' said the cock sparrowhawk, not at all pleased. 'What are you doing here, tawny owl? We have made this hole ours, and we shall soon start building in this old squirrel's nest.'

'This is a good hole,' said the owl, stretching out his claws. 'I am always going to roost here in the daytime. You may have it at night, if you

like, because I hunt when it is dark and shall not
need it then.'

'What! Both of us share this hole!' cried the
hawks, indignantly. 'You must be mad. We
don't want our young ones eaten by *you*.'

'I prefer mice or rats,' said the owl. 'Look at
my great claws. When I catch a mouse my talons
curve round and make a kind of trap.'

'I don't mind a mouse myself,' said the cock
sparrowhawk, looking at the owl's cruel claws.
'But I should be afraid to catch a rat. Rats have
such sharp teeth, and might bite my legs.'

'Then you should wear feathered leggings as
I do,' said the owl, and the sparrowhawk saw
that his legs were feathered thickly right down
to the feet to protect his legs from bites.

'That is certainly a good idea,' said the sparrowhawk, looking sadly at his own bare legs.
'Tell me, owl, why do you hunt at night, when
it is too dark to see anything.'

'I can always see in the dark!' said the owl,
opening his big round eyes very wide indeed.
'So could you if you had eyes like mine. My
wings are very soft and silent, so that I can fly
just above a rat and he will not hear me till I
pounce.'

Just as the sparrowhawk was going to answer,
a big, whitish shape came floating silently down

to the oak tree in the darkness, and then there came a most terrifying screech – so frightening that the two hawks almost fell off the tree in terror.

'Hoo hoo hoo!' laughed the tawny owl from his hole in the tree. 'Good evening, cousin. You certainly have a fine voice.'

'It's the screech owl,' said the cock sparrow-hawk to his frightened mate. 'You know – the barn owl that we sometimes see roosting in the old shed down at the farm.'

'Good hunting, cousin!' called the barn owl, his great eyes peering in at the hollow. 'I heard you were roosting here. Come out, for there are plenty of mice about tonight. What are you doing here? Is it a good roosting place?'

'Yes,' said the tawny owl, clambering out of the hole. 'You should try it, cousin. These hawks want to nest here, and I have told them that so long as I can use it in the daytime they can have it for a nesting place as well.'

The barn owl screeched again, and all the mice in the hedgerow below sank down as still as stones in the grass, terrified. The hawks were startled, for it was a noise that no bird or animal could ever get used to, it was so weird and horrifying.

'Cousin, you are clever,' said the barn owl,

swinging his head slowly round and staring at the two sparrowhawks. 'You like a *larder* in your roosting place!'

'Hoo, hoo, hoo!' hooted the tawny owl, laughing loudly. The two sparrowhawks were angry and afraid. They were fierce birds themselves, but they did not like the look of the queer cat-like owls, with their strange hootings and terrible screeches.

The tawny owl spread his big wings, and suddenly flew off over the hedgerow, keeping a sharp lookout as he went for the tiniest movement in the grass below, which would show him where a mouse ran. His wings were quite silent, his big eyes were wide open, and he was able to see all he needed in the darkness of the night.

The cock sparrowhawk went to the hollow in the oak tree and peered in. He did not like to roost there now. It was spoilt for him. Just as he was about to hop back to his mate the barn owl screeched again, almost in his ear. The sparrowhawk was so startled that he fell right into the squirrel's old nest, and it was a minute or two before he came out again, angry and ruffled, to his anxious mate.

'Let us go, said the cock. 'These bad-mannered owls would disturb us too much if we nested here. I have remembered an old nest in the pine wood that will do for us to build in. Let us fly there to roost before that owl screeches again.'

But the barn owl was gone on silent wings, for his sharp eyes had seen a movement over in the field – a rat hunting for food. The sparrow-hawks flew off, too, and were soon lost in the shadows of the night.

From underneath the squirrel's nest crept a small mouse, after he had listened for some time, and was sure the hawks and owls were not there. He had been hiding in terror there all the day. He had heard all that was said – and now he was anxious to spread the glad news that the hawks were not going to nest in the old oak tree after all. He crept down the oak tree and squeaked out his news.

'The hawks are gone! We are safe! They are not nesting here after all. But beware the owls – they are about tonight. Beware the owls!'

Soon every bird and every small creature had heard the news. They kept close to their holes and hiding places that night, but all of them rejoiced to know that the hawks were gone. As for the sparrows, they talked about it at the tops of their voices all the next day, till the blackbird came and scolded them well for making such a noise. But even that didn't stop their chatter!

The Wonderful Traveller

In the pond that lay by the alder trees lived a long, strange creature, greenish-brown in colour, with a sharp snout and large eyes. It was a big eel, wise and much travelled, clever at hiding itself in the mud, and sharp at catching unwary fish or newts. Summer and winter it lived in the pond, sometimes leaving it to go for a short journey along the bottom of the ditch when it was muddy and wet. At the sight of the long, thick creature wriggling along the frogs and toads froze with terror, for it was seldom that they saw the eel in their ditch.

The old toad who had lived under the hedgerow and spawned in the pond for many years knew the eel better than any other creature knew him. He had seen him come to the pond years before! The old toad had seen many strange things and watched scores of curious happenings with his bright, coppery eyes. He was the oldest of the hedgerow creatures, older even than the badger who sometimes came sniffing along the hedge on a warm night. He often sat and remembered all he had seen and heard, his eyes closed and his body squat, looking for all the world like a lump of earth!

It was whilst the toad was in the pond with his mate that he saw the eel again. First he saw a mist of mud rise up in the water near a big stone at the bottom. The toad knew that this meant some creature was under the stone, and he swam hurriedly to another stone he knew, and crept under it with his mate. As he watched from his hiding place he saw the eel wriggle out from under his big stone and dart at an unwary frog. A little water-vole, whose home had an entrance under the water not far from the toad's hiding place, called out to the toad:

'That's the end of that frog! He was always foolish! He was nearly eaten last week by the duck, and yesterday the heron nearly caught him. Now he is quite gone.'

'Only the strongest or wisest of us live a long life,' said the toad, blinking his eyes. 'I am very old.'

'Are you older than the eel?' asked the water vole.

'I was here when he came,' said the toad. 'But

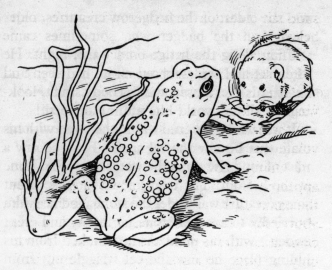

he was different then. He was much smaller, and his snout was broad, not sharp. His eyes were smaller too. He was not nearly so long as he is now, nor so thick in the body – but that was six years ago! I have watched him change and grow. He came here one spring morning. I remember it quite well.'

'Tell me about it,' begged the little water vole, who dearly loved a good story.

'I had finished spawning that year,' said the toad, shutting his eyes and trying to remember everything. 'I was squatting on the hedge bank in a rain shower, enjoying the drops on my back, not far from my stone there. I suddenly heard a strange noise in the ditch below.'

'What was it?' asked the water vole.

'I looked down,' said the toad. 'It wasn't a shuffling hedgehog. It wasn't a leaping frog. It wasn't a sliding snake. It was – the eel!'

'Where had he come from?' asked the water vole in surprise.

'I don't know,' said the toad. 'He just appeared from somewhere. He wriggled along the damp ditch and I followed him on the bank above, for I had never seen an eel before. He came at last to the pond and slid into it. He was only a little creature then, thin and half-transparent. But, as you see, he has grown long and strong, and is an enemy to all small creatures who live in or near the water. He has never found a wife, has never laid any eggs or had young ones. He is a strange, lonely creature.'

The eel swam up to the toad's stone, and at once the water vole disappeared into his hole in a great hurry. The toad did not move. He knew that the eel could not reach him, so he sat and looked at the long creature, marvelling at his great length.

'I heard what you said to the vole,' said the eel. 'You do not know everything, old toad. You are right when you say that I am a strange creature, but even you, wise though you are, could not even begin to guess the strange and wonderful life I have led, the long journeys I have made, and the long travels I have still to make! You are an old stay-at-home – I have travelled half across the world, and I shall do so again!'

The toad did not believe the eel.

'You are a boaster,' he said. 'You are like the frogs. They say they have been to the moon and back when they see it shining in a puddle!'

The eel was angry. It lashed its long tail and made little waves on the top of the pond.

'Listen to me,' it said. 'I was born thousands of miles away in the depths of an ocean.'

'What is an ocean?' asked the toad in surprise. 'Is it like this pond?'

'It is endless water!' said the eel. 'It is deep, so deep, and there are thousands of weird and marvellous creatures living in its depths, besides many beautiful fish. I have seen them all. I hatched out of an egg nine years ago, so I am old, very old. I was a strange looking creature then, and knew little.'

'What were you like?' asked the toad, curiously.

'I was leaf-like in shape,' said the eel, trying to remember, 'and very thin – as thin as that sheet of brown paper that once lay by the pond-side. I am as long and round as a pipe now, I know, but in those days I was flat and you could have seen right through me, for I was transparent. I swam about for a while in the deep ocean and then I and many many thousands of other silvery eels began to swim to the north-east – and after about three years I came to land! I had changed on the way. I became smaller, and my body lost its flat shape and became rounder as it is now.'

'What did you do next?' asked the toad, his eyes nearly bulging out of his head with wonder at this strange story.

'I left the salt seawater and swam up a big river,' said the eel. 'Many companions were with me. We swam up in a great shoal. Then gradually our company broke up. Some entered small streams. Some swam to a lake. I found the ditch out there by the hedgerow. It was full of water then from the spring rains, and it led me to this pond. Here I have been ever since, growing bigger and longer each year. Ah, you should have seen me in that long journey, toad! Once we came to a lock-gate, and it was shut – so we scrambled over it! And another time we came to a rushing waterfall, which, every time we tried to clamber up, knocked us down again. So we wriggled our way up the old moss-grown stones by the side of the waterfall. It was a great adventure.'

'Shall you stay here always?' asked the toad. 'What will happen if you grow bigger and bigger and bigger? The pond will not hold you!'

'The time is nearly come when I must go again,' said the eel. 'I felt last December that I must go, for the ditches then were moist and easy to journey through, and the streams were full and rushed to the sea – so I started out, but I was caught in an eel-trap and hurt my back. Then I came back here again to my pond to get better. But now I must soon go, for I have lost my greenish-brown colouring and have become silvery. All eels must go back to the salt sea when they become old. They must find wives and must lay their eggs in the deep ocean so that there may be thousands of other young eels to follow them. It will take me many months to reach my birthplace and I must go before I die.'

'Well, your tale is wonderful,' said the toad, his throat swelling with a loud croak. 'But I shall not be sorry to say goodbye to you, eel, for you have many a time tried to catch me, and you must have eaten hundreds of us in your life.'

'I would not eat a wise old toad like you,' promised the eel.

'You might not know it was I until you had swallowed me,' said the toad, wisely, quite

determined not to move from his safe hiding place.

Suddenly the eel twisted his head round and stared in amazement at a small creature which had just wriggled up to him. The toad stretched out his head to have a look. He saw another eel – but very, very small indeed.

'Where do you come from?' cried the large eel in delight and amazement.

'From the deep seas,' answered the small creature, who was so transparent that he looked as if he might almost be made of glass. 'I was born there, as you were, cousin. It has taken me three years and more to get to this pond. Is there good hunting here?'

'Plenty of everything,' answered the eel, swimming round his small cousin in delight. 'See how I have grown on the fare here. I am surely the biggest eel you have met on your journeys.'

'Oh, I have met far bigger eels than you,' said the small eel. 'Why did you not leave your pond earlier, cousin? You are old, and you should not leave your last long journey till you are weak, for it is a very long way. You may die before you get to our birthplace.'

'I shall go this very day,' said the big eel. 'Most of the old eels went in the autumn, I know, but we have had much rain lately, and the streams are full of water. It will be easy for me to swim down with the current, and I shall soon reach the sea.'

'Beware of eel-traps, cousin,' warned the small eel. 'We elvers escaped them, for we are very small – you are big.'

The eel called goodbye to the little elver and swam to the ditch that led into the pond. He

70

wriggled into it and saw the old toad sitting high up on the bank, watching.

'Goodbye!' cried the eel. 'I go on my long journey back to the depths of the ocean again.'

'You are a wonderful traveller!' called back the toad. 'Goodbye! It is a pity you cannot take your small cousin with you. He will be just as much danger to us when he grows, as *you* have been. Goodbye – and good riddance!'

But the eel did not hear. He had left the pond and the hedgerow behind him for ever.

Creepy Creatures

One bright sunny morning, when the birds were busy taking food to their young ones in the hedgerow, and the little mice were scuttling about in their secret passages under the grasses, the blackbird gave his rattling cry of alarm.

'Beware! An enemy! I see him in the ditch! Beware!'

At the first notes of the blackbird's cry all the little birds fell silent and those sitting on their nest crouched very still. The mice shot into their holes and stayed there. The big toad who was crawling along at the bottom of the ditch squatted perfectly still as if he had frozen to the ground. The hedgehog on the bank stood still and peered down into the ditch below.

'It's only a snake!' he called to the toad. 'Who's afraid of a grass snake? I'm not!'

'Well, I'm not either,' said the toad, though he was really. 'I can make myself taste horrible, so that if a snake picks me up in his mouth he has to spit me out again!'

'Sssssssss!' came the voice of the long grass snake in the ditch. 'Sssssssss!'

The snake raised his head, and looked around him with his gold-gleaming eyes. He was olive-green and very long, over four feet in length. He had a graceful, tapering tail, and from his mouth there darted out his black, forked tongue. But behind his head he had bright orange patches that looked like a collar.

A small rabbit, peeping through the hedge, saw the snake's black tongue, and shivered.

'Is that its sting?' he asked an older rabbit.

'Sting!' said the rabbit, scornfully, 'don't be so ignorant! That's only a tongue. The snake uses it to feel things. I've often seen that snake run its tongue over something. But it darts it in and out like that just to frighten us. Don't be afraid of that snake, youngster; it won't harm you. You're too big. It can only eat things by swallowing them, and it could never swallow *you*, you're too fat!'

'But don't snakes sting?' asked the fat young rabbit. 'I'm sure they do! I've heard the frogs say so.'

'Don't listen to those stupid creatures,' said the old rabbit. 'There's a snake that *bites* most poisonously, but that's not the grass snake yonder. *He* has no poison in his fangs. He's quite harmless to us. It's the adder that bites, but he's quite different from the grass snake.'

'Where does the adder . . .' began the little fat rabbit – but he didn't finish what he was saying, for the old rabbit suddenly gave a thump with his hind feet, shot round and dived for his burrow. The little rabbit saw his white bobtail jerking up and down, a signal for him to run too. He rushed to his hole, and then, turning round, looked out to see what all the excitement was.

He saw another snake gliding over the grass towards the hedgerow, and at the same moment the blackbird gave another loud cry.

'An adder! An adder! Beware, you folk of the hedgerow!'

The grass snake heard the blackbird's cry and looked towards the adder. 'Good day, cousin,' he said, surprised. 'Why have you left the warm common and come to this damp ditch?'

'I have a fancy for a frog-meal,' said the adder, his short black tongue flickering in and out. 'I have fed on lizards for the past week, and I need a change.'

'I am not so sure I like your company,' said the grass snake.

'Why is that?' asked the adder, his coppery eyes gleaming angrily. 'I will not harm you.'

'I know that,' said the grass snake. 'But I am

so often mistaken for you that I am quite afraid of knowing you. You are poisonous, you know, and the two-legged folk kill you. I am not poisonous. I am quite harmless, a gentle and friendly creature, and I dislike being mistaken for a fierce creature like you.'

'There is no reason why any one should mistake you for me!' said the adder, disbelievingly. 'Look at us! We are quite different! I am only two feet long and you are much longer. I am thick and stocky, and you are graceful and tapering. And look at the large scales on your head! Mine are very small, and I never wear your orange or white collar.'

'And I never wear the strange mark you bear on your head!' said the grass snake, staring at the V-shaped black mark on the adder's blunt head. 'I do wish people would learn the differences between us, then I could be friendly with them instead of going in fear of my life!'

The adder thought it was time to change the subject. 'Where did you pass the winter?' he asked.

'I found a warm place deep down under the roots of this old oak tree,' said the snake. 'I slept well, and awoke when I heard the frogs croaking in the pond some weeks ago.'

'I have only been awake for a few days,' said

the adder, yawning. 'I found a great heap of bracken up on the hill and I curled up with two of my brothers at the very bottom of it. It was most comfortable.'

'Let us hunt for a meal,' begged the grass snake, who was very hungry. 'I shall go to the pond and swim a little. There are so many frogs there now.'

'I will come with you,' said the adder. 'Perhaps I shall find a frog on the bank of the pond.'

The two snakes glided off together, and the hedgehog lifted up his voice and called rudely after them. The snakes stopped in anger. They hissed and their tongues flickered in and out. The hedgehog showed himself and began to amble towards them. He was not at all afraid.

'I like a snake for a meal! I like a snake for a meal!' he called. The snakes looked at him for a moment and then glided quickly towards the pond.

'He is a nasty little creature,' said the adder, looking back. 'I have often tried to bite him, but he does not seem to mind my poison. He has a curious armour of spines, and he is so fearless that he will even attack me if I give him the chance.'

'We will take no notice of him,' said the grass snake. 'See, here is the pond.'

He slipped into the water and swam swiftly here and there, darting at the unwary frogs. He caught one and came to the bank with it in his mouth. He lay down in the sun and began to swallow the poor creature. It could not get away because the hooked, backward-pointing teeth inside the snake's mouth held it too tightly.

Meantime the adder had spied a fat newt. He darted his head forward like lightning and caught the newt in his jaws. The grass snake saw his fangs stand erect as he struck, and knew that poison had been pressed into the poor newt's body. It was killed by the poison and the hungry adder swallowed the lifeless creature eagerly.

Both snakes lay in the hot sun, digesting their meal. They lay so still that a big toad, crawling

towards the pond, did not see them. He thought
they were part of the bank of the pond.

But the grass snake saw *him*. As the slow toad
passed by the snake slid back his head a little
and then struck. The toad saw the snake's head
coming and in a trice he poured out an evil-
tasting, evil-smelling liquid over his warty back.
The snake tasted this when the toad was in his
mouth and in the greatest disgust dropped his
prey hurriedly. The wily creature lay still for a
moment and then began to crawl away.

The snake lowered its head again and struck
once more, for he could not bear to see the toad

escaping. But once again the evil taste forced him to drop the toad, and this time the slow crawling creature managed to reach the pond, drop into the water, and swim swiftly to safety.

'Did you see that?' cried the watching blackbird, who had not let the snake out of his sight. 'The toad escaped. I saw him. I saw him!'

'You talk too much !' the adder hissed, looking savagely at the glossy blackbird on the nearby bough. 'If you are not silent I will find your nest and eat your young ones!'

The blackbird flew off, alarmed. The snakes basked happily in the hot April sun. A small mouse ran out to look at the curious heap on the bank and at once the adder snapped him up. He gave a pitiful squeal and disappeared.

'See what happens to foolish children!' squeaked all the mice who dwelt nearby, to their trembling young ones.

'That toad tasted horrible,' said the grass snake to the adder. 'I must eat something else to get the taste out of my mouth.'

'I have known *you* to smell even worse than that toad tasted!' said the adder, uncoiling himself to stare at his companion. 'Do you remember the time that a man caught you and was going to kill you? You made yourself smell so horrible that he dropped you and you took the chance to escape.'

'That man thought I was *you*,' said the grass snake, indignantly. 'I cannot defend myself as you can. I have no poison fangs – so the only thing I could do was to make myself disgusting. That is what I was saying to you before – I am always suffering because I am mistaken for you. I wish you would go away and never come near me.'

'I will very soon,' said the adder. 'But first I have something to do that cannot wait. I must change my skin! It has already split round my mouth and is most uncomfortable.'

The grass snake watched him. The adder rubbed his head against a stone to loosen his skin. Then, very gradually, the whole of his scaly skin peeled off, and the adder was able to glide out of it, leaving it turned inside out like a stocking! He was shining new, and proud of himself.

'I shall go to find a wife now that I am so handsome,' he called to the grass snake, as he glided off.

'Where will she lay her eggs?' called the grass snake after him. 'I shall put mine in that heap of manure at the end of the field, so do not have yours laid there!'

'*We* do not lay eggs!' called the adder, scornfully. 'Our young ones come from the eggs as they are dropped by the mother adder. Didn't you know *that*?'

The grass snake made no answer. He glided away swiftly, and the blackbird cried out the glad news.

'The hedgerow is safe! The snakes are gone! All clear, friends, all clear!'

The Blue Visitor

The pond that lay quietly near the hedgerow was always a very busy place. The frogs croaked there, and the newts swam about in the water. The wild ducks sometimes came, and the slow-flying heron, with his deep voice calling 'Kronk! Kronk!' The snakes hunted for fish in the water, swimming gracefully, and most of the birds drank from the edge. So did the hedgerow animals – some in daylight, but most of them at night.

King of the pond was the little black moor-hen, with his bobbing, red-marked head and long dark green legs. He lived there all the year round, feeding on fish, tadpoles, water weeds and anything else he could pick up for a living. He said 'Fulluck! Fulluck!' in the reeds, and the hedgerow folk knew him very well indeed. He could run as fast as he could swim, and some-times he spread his wings and flew off to the farm away in the distance to have a meal of grain.

The year before he had had a nice little wife, but she had been caught by a cunning fox and killed. So when the springtime came and the moorhen wanted a nest, there was no little mate to help him to build one. 'Fulluck! Fulluck!' he said to himself as he swam across the pond, bobbing his perky little head.

'Where shall I find a mate? The primroses are here, the sky is blue as the little speedwell on the bank, it is springtime – but I have no one to make love to!'

That day a visitor came to the pond. It was a kingfisher, gleaming blue and green in the sunshine. He was rather a stumpy bird to look at, with a long strong beak, and a short tail – but he was beautiful in his colouring! His chestnut breast shone, his back was like the sky, and his head and wings gleamed a marvellous green as he turned here and there. The moorhen gaped at him in envy. *He* was black, sober black, with the front of his head and base of his bill a bright red – a dull creature compared with the brilliance of the kingfisher!

The kingfisher was friendly. He sat on an alder branch that stretched over the pond and looked for fish in the water below. He called

'Kee kee kee!' to the moorhen and the moorhen answered at once: 'Fulluck! Fulluck!'

'You will find more fish if you come down and swim on the water,' said the moorhen. 'That is how I catch *my* fish!'

'And this is how I catch *mine*!' called the kingfisher, diving into the water like an arrow. He came up with a fish wriggling in his mouth; He held it crossways. He knocked it sharply against the alder branch and killed it. Then he swallowed it, head first.

'Very clever,' said the moorhen, admiringly. 'I wish I could do that.'

'Do you happen to know of a good hole on the banks of this pond where I could nest?' asked the kingfisher. 'This seems to be a fine pond for fish. It would be a good place to bring up my young ones. I have a beautiful little wife and we are looking for a place to nest in.'

'Yes!' said the moorhen, eagerly. 'There is a fine hole in the bank over by the hedgerow there, at the end of the pond. It once belonged to a water vole. Would that do, do you think?'

The kingfisher flew down to the hole and went inside. He soon came out, excited and pleased.

'Just the thing!' he cried. 'I shall fetch my wife and bring her to live here. I am so glad I visited this pond today!'

'Do you know of a little moorhen who would like to come and live with me and build a nest?' called the moorhen.

'I'll see!' said the kingfisher, and off he flew. The next day he was back again with his wife, who was just as brilliant as he was. How excited she was to see the hole in the bank! It did not go quite far enough in, so the two birds busily dug it farther back until they had made a tunnel quite three feet long. It sloped upwards a little to prevent the rain from running in. The moorhen went to see the hole, and the kingfisher told him that he was going to make a nest at the end of it.

'I forgot to tell you something,' he said. 'I saw a moorhen yesterday on the river and she would like to come and live with you. She will soon be here.'

The moorhen was very much excited to hear this. He preened his wings and made them glossy. He swam all round the pond crying 'Fulluck! Fulluck! I shall soon have a wife!' He looked carefully for a good place in which to nest.

The little moorhen came the next day. She was a timid little thing, but pretty and good-natured. The moorhen was delighted with her. He showed her all round the pond and she thought it very comfortable and well stocked with food.

'Here is where I thought we might build our nest,' said the moorhen, showing his mate some thick rushes. She agreed at once. And then, what a happy time they had, the two of them! They were so pleased with one another, so glad to be together in the sunny days of early summer! The kingfishers too were very happy. They had made their home in the hole on the bank, and to it they often took the moorhens to show them how comfortable it was. But after a while the moorhens didn't like it. They said it smelt horrible.

So it did! For in the tunnel there were now a great many old fishbones and fishy pellets that the kingfishers had thrown up after digesting the fish they had eaten. These smelt nasty as they decayed, and the two moorhens could not bear the smell. But the kingfishers didn't mind. Fish was fish whether bad or good, and the smell seemed quite natural to them.

One day the cock kingfisher called excitedly to the moorhens: 'Kee kee kee! Come and see! We have a nest and eggs now!'

So the moorhens went to see. They peered into the smelly tunnel, and saw the nest at the end – and it was made of old fishbones! 'What

a nest for young ones to hatch on!' thought the
cleanly moorhens, in disgust. There were five
round eggs, and they gleamed white in the
darkness of the tunnel. The mother kingfisher
sat down proudly on her eggs again, settling
herself comfortably on the fishbones.

'Come and see *our* nest now!' said the
moorhens to the kingfisher. They swam off and
the kingfisher followed. Certainly the moorhens' nest was a nice open-air affair after
the smelly one in the tunnel. It was a plat-
form made of flattened out rushes, and it was
right on the water itself. In the middle the plat-
form sank a little to hold the eggs. There were
seven eggs there, buff-coloured with red spots,

and they were large compared with the king-fishers'.

'It doesn't seem a very *safe* nest to me,' said the kingfisher, doubtfully. 'Why, anyone could see it!'

'But nobody *has*!' said the moorhen as she clambered up to the platform and sat on her eggs.

In the lovely summertime the moorhens' eggs hatched out into amusing little chicks. The king-fisher's eggs hatched too, but nobody saw the young ones for some time, for they were well hidden in the tunnel. Everyone knew the moorhens' little black chicks, for before two weeks had passed they were swimming merrily about the pond, seven little black dobs with jerk-ing heads! They followed their father and mother everywhere, and if either of their parents gave the alarm cry and scuttled over the water hurriedly to the reeds, the youngsters would see the white underparts of their parents' tails gleaming brightly and would follow quickly to a safe hiding place.

Each little bird had a hook-claw on one wing and when they needed to climb up to the plat-form nest they used this claw as a hand and could reach the nest easily. But one day when they climbed up, what a surprise! There were more eggs in the nest!

'You cannot sleep in the nest now,' said their father. 'I will build you another one nearby. Your mother needs the nest for her second family. You must help her now all you can.'

The little creatures settled happily down on the new nest, and were most excited when the second batch of eggs hatched out. 'Crek, crek!' cried one. 'I will go and find some food for our tiny brothers and sisters!'

Off went all the youngsters eagerly, and soon came back with titbits for the new family. By the next day there were seventeen moorhens – the two parents, seven of the first family, and eight new youngsters, who belonged to the second batch of eggs! How full the pond seemed! What a happy time all the little black moor-chicks had, swimming about, calling to one another, bobbing here and there, diving to the bottom, finding food for themselves and the babies – and even helping to make another nest in case their mother laid a third batch of eggs! They were a very happy and contented family.

The chicks were taught many things, and the chief lesson was how to swim under water to escape an enemy. Their mother was very clever at this. She would bob down under the water and swim across the pond without showing herself at all. Then, at the other side, she would

just put her red-marked bill above the water,
and nothing else. All the chicks practised this
until they too could swim across the pond under
water.

The moorhens were so busy with their two
families that they forgot all about the kingfishers – and then one morning, what a surprise! They saw five small kingfishers all sitting
on an alder branch over the water, having their
first lesson in fishing! The little kingfishers were
proud and excited. They had often peeped out
of their hole, but they had never fished for
themselves before.

'Kee, kee, kee!' called their father, and he
dived in to show them how to catch a fish. He
flew up to the branch with a gleaming fish in his
beak, but he would not give it to any of the
hungry youngsters. He threw it back into the
pond and it floated there, dead. 'Go and get it if
you want it!' cried the kingfisher.

The five small kingfishers looked down
hungrily. One of them suddenly opened his
wings, dropped down to the water and snatched
up the fish. Back to the branch he flew, excited
and pleased. He ate the fish and looked down for
another.

'Good!' said his father. 'Now try to catch a live
fish, or even a fat tadpole. But remember this –

knock your fish hard against a branch when you
have caught it, for it is unpleasant to swallow a
wriggling creature – and *always* swallow it head
first, never tail first or it might stick in your
throat!'

'But suppose we catch it tail-first,' said a
youngster. 'What shall we do?'

'I'll show you!' said the father and he dived in
and caught another fish, this time tail first. He
knocked it against a branch, threw it up into the
air, neatly caught it *head* first and swallowed it!

One by one the youngsters dived into the
water and soon learnt how to catch fish for
themselves. The moorhens enjoyed watching
them. And then one day all the kingfishers
called goodbye.

'Kee kee kee!' said the old kingfishers. 'There
will not be enough food in this small pond for all
you moorhens and so many kingfishers. So I am
taking my family to the big river where there is
more food than a hundred kingfishers can catch.
Goodbye! Kee kee kee!'

'Fulluck, fulluck!' cried all the moorhens at
once. The kingfishers flew off, seven bright
streaks of blue, and, although the moorhens saw
them no more, they often heard them calling to
one another from the river. 'Kee kee kee! Kee
kee kee!'

The Little Fawn

For days the sun had shone from a cloudless sky, and the oak leaves hung dry and dusty on the tree. The poppies flaunted their red frocks at the fieldside, throwing off their tight green caps in the early morning, and flinging down their red petals at night, as if they were really too hot to wear anything at all. Butterflies of all kinds came to the pink and white bramble flowers on the hedgerow, and wasps and bees hummed from dawn to dusk.

The hedgerow was thirsty. The grass beneath was parched and brown. Everything wanted the cool rain. The pond water fell lower and lower, and the fish began to be anxious. What would happen if they had no water to swim in? The moorhens talked of going to the big river, but they were fond of the little pond and stayed.

And then, late one afternoon the rain came. Great purple-black clouds sailed up from the southwest and covered all the sky. It seemed very dark after the brilliance of the summer sun.

Then suddenly a flash of bright lightning tore the sky in half, and the startled birds flew to the hedge for shelter. Almost at once there came a loud peal of thunder that rolled round the sky, and sent the young rabbits scampering back to their burrows in fright.

And then, what a downpour! First came big drops that made wide round ripples on the pond, and set the oak-tree leaves dancing up and down. Then came a deluge of smaller drops, beating down faster and faster. The old toad crawled out from his stone and lay in the rainstorm, his mouth opening and shutting in delight as he felt the rain trickling down his back. Crowds of young frogs jumped out of the pond and hopped to the ditch for joy. The hedgehog found a sheltered place and curled up in disgust, for he didn't like the way the rain ran down his prickles. It tickled him.

Soon a delicious smell arose from the field and hedge – the smell of the rain sinking into the earth. All the animals sniffed it. It was good. In their ears sounded the rippling and gurgling, the splashing and the dripping of the rain. They heard every plant drinking greedily. They heard the excited moorhens scuttling in the rain over the pond. It was a glorious time.

The clouds grew blacker. The lightning flashed again and the thunder growled and grumbled like a great bear in the sky – and just as the storm was at its height there came the sound of tiny galloping hooves. They sounded through the pattering of the rain, and all the rabbits heard them and peeped out of their holes, the rain wetting their fine whiskers. The toad heard them too and crawled back quickly to his hole. He did not wish to be tramped on.

The newcomer ran to the hedgerow and stopped there in its shelter. It was a small fawn, a baby deer, only a few weeks old. The hedgerow was surprised, for it had never seen a fawn before.

The little fawn was trembling in all its limbs. Its soft eyes were wide with fright, and its tail swung to and fro. Another peal of thunder sounded overhead, beginning with a noise like a giant clapping of hands. The fawn closed its eyes in terror and sank down on the grass.

It was frightened of the storm. Its mother had left it safely hidden in the bracken of the distant wood, and had bade it stay there until she returned. But then the storm had come, and the little fawn, who had never seen lightning before, or heard thunder, had been terrified. The jays in the wood had screamed in delight at the rain, and the fawn had thought they were screeching in terror. Fear had filled his small, beating heart and he had run from his hiding place, through the wood, across the fields – anywhere, anywhere, to get away from this dreadful noise and terrible flashing light.

But the storm seemed to follow him. The rain came and lashed him, beating into his eyes. The thunder rolled exactly above his head – or so it seemed to him. Where was his mother? Why did she not come to him? He was so frightened that his legs would no longer carry him and he sank down on the grass beside the old hedgerow.

He made a little bleating sound and the old mother rabbit, who had heard many young animals crying for their mother, looked out of a hole nearby. She saw the frightened fawn and was sorry for him. She ran out of her burrow in the rain and went up to the panting fawn.

'Don't be afraid,' she said. 'It is only a thunderstorm. It will pass. Be glad of the good rain, little creature, and lick it from the grass. It will taste good.'

The fawn looked at the soft-eyed rabbit and was comforted. It was good to see another creature near him, one that was not frightened. He put out his hot tongue and licked the wet grass. The raindrops were cool and sweet. He stopped trembling and lay calmly in the rain.

'Come under the hedgerow,' said the rabbit. 'You will get wet lying there. This hedgerow is thick and will shelter you well till the storm is past.'

The little fawn obediently pushed his way into the hedge and lay down in the dry, though he could easily reach the dripping grass with his pink tongue.

'Where do you come from?' asked the rabbit, inquisitively. 'I have never seen you before, though I have heard my mother tell of creatures like you in the woods.'

'I am a young fallow deer,' said the fawn, looking at the rabbit out of his beautiful big eyes. 'I was born this summer. I live in the wood with my mother, and I have a fine hiding place there among the high bracken. There is no bracken here, or I would show you how well I can hide underneath the big green fronds.'

'Bracken is good for hiding in,' said the rabbit. 'Where are your antlers, little fawn? I thought deer had antlers growing out from their head.'

'I have none yet,' said the fawn. 'But next year they will begin to grow. They will look like two horns at first, but in the second year they will grow more like antlers and every year they will grow bigger and bigger, until I am full-grown and show great antlers such as I have seen on my father's head.'

'Surely those big antlers are a nuisance to you in the woods?' said the rabbit, in surprise. 'Don't they catch in the tree branches as you run?'

'No,' said the fawn. 'We throw our heads backwards as we run, and then our antlers lie along our sides and do not catch in anything. Also they protect our bodies from any scratches or bruises we might get as we run through the trees and bushes. My mother has no antlers – but she has told me that I shall grow some soon.'

'Do you wear them all the year round?' asked the rabbit.

'Oh, no,' said the fawn. 'They drop off in the springtime and then grow again in a few weeks. On my head I have two little bumps, and it is from these I shall grow my antlers each year. My father has wonderful antlers, very large and spreading, and they show what a great age he is. But he will drop his antlers next springtime, and they will have to grow again from the knobs on his forehead. That is what my mother told me.'

'How strange!' said the rabbit, in astonishment, looking at the little dappled fawn as he lay under the hedge. 'What do you eat, little creature?'

'Oh, I eat grass and toadstools and the shoots of young trees,' said the fawn, beginning to feel hungry. 'And often we eat the bark of trees. I should like something to eat now.'

'There are some turnips in the field on the other side of the hedge,' said the rabbit. 'Would you like some?'

The fawn did not know what turnips were, but he jumped to his feet and followed the rabbit, squeezing himself through the hedge. The storm was over now, but the rain still fell gently. The thunder was muttering far away over the hills, but there was no longer any lightning. Blue sky began to appear between the ragged clouds and once the sun peeped through.

All the hedgerow was hung with twinkling raindrops. The oak tree shone brilliantly, for every one of its leaves had been well washed by the rain. The fawn slipped into the turnip field and began to nibble at the young turnips. They were delicious.

When he had eaten enough he went back to the hedgerow. The rabbit followed him and told him that he should go back to the woods, for his mother would be anxious about him – and at that very moment the blackbird in the tree above sent out his alarm cry.

'Kukka-kuk! Beware! Here comes a strange enemy!'

Every animal scuttled back to its hole, and all

the birds flew to the topmost branches. The little fawn stood up and smelt the air. Suddenly he made a strange, welcoming sound and rushed up to the newcomer. It was his mother, a big, well-grown deer, with soft eyes and small, neat feet with cloven hooves.

She nuzzled her fawn in delight. She had missed him from his hiding place and had come to seek him.

'Come,' she said to him. 'You should not have run away, little fawn. Enemies might have seen you and captured you. You are safe under the bracken in the woods.'

'But a loud and flashing enemy came,' said the fawn, rubbing himself against his mother lovingly. 'I was afraid.'

'That was only a storm,' said his mother.

'There are good turnips in the field over there,' said the little fawn. 'I have eaten some.'

'We will stay under this hedge until the dark comes,' said the deer. 'Then we will feast on the turnips before we return to the woods. Let us find a dry place.'

Under the thick ivy was a big, dry patch, for the ivy leaves made a dense shelter there. The deer lay down with her fawn beside her and they waited until evening came. They lay so quiet that none of the hedgerow folk feared them, and the little mice, the hedgehog and the toad went about their business just as usual.

After they had fed on the sweet turnips the little fawn called goodbye to the old rabbit who had been so kind, and then in the soft blue evening time the two trotted back to the woodlands.

'Come again!' called the rabbits, who liked the gentle deer. 'Come again and share our turnips!'

The Fish that Built a Nest

In the pond that lay near the hedgerow lived many fish. Some were tiny, like the sticklebacks. Some were bigger, like the carp and the bream. The sticklebacks often swam in shoals, darting here and there in the sunny patches of water, happily playing together. It was safer to swim in a shoal than to swim alone. If a small fish swam by himself an enemy could see him and chase him until he was caught – but if he swam in a shoal an enemy might be too afraid to chase such numbers of fish; and even if he did there were so many fish in a shoal that it was a hundred chances to one he would be caught!

The fish loved to feel the hot summer sun on the pond. They swam in the warm water, looking for tiny insects, darting at the grubs of gnats, chasing the little water fleas and swallowing them whole. There was always plenty of food on the pond.

One small stickleback, with three sharp spines on his back, was very happy that summer. He had been well fed and he was strong and fierce. He knew all the creatures of the pond, and he knew too which to keep away from, and which were harmless and interesting to talk to. He liked the small frogs and the great big water beetle. He liked the little water spider who had made a marvellous home of silvery water bubbles neatly tied by silken ropes to the stems of water reeds. At first he had tried to catch her and eat her, but she was too clever for him. She would dart at once to her bubble-nest and squeeze into it. She was quite safe there, for the tiny fish did not like to feel his head caught

103

in the silken threads around it. He had seen water insects caught in that webbing, and eaten by the spider!

Once he made a terrible mistake that nearly cost him his life. He had become friendly with the great water beetle who swam clumsily about in the warm water, biting the water weed and the stems of juicy plants. He would often swim by him and watch him, and never tired of hearing how the water beetle could, if he wished, go to the top of the water, spread his hidden wings, and fly up into the air above. This seemed wonderful to the little fish. He had once tried to jump out of the water to see what it was like to be in the world above, and he had landed on a waterlily leaf and lain there, gasping for breath. Happily he had managed to jerk himself back into the water again, and had swum to a hole, trembling with fright.

One day he thought he saw his friend the great black water beetle, so he swam up to him to ask him where he had been. His friend seemed much smaller and the little stickleback stared at him in surprise. Then, to his astonishment and dismay, the beetle darted at him and nearly caught him!

It was not his friend after all, but it was the smaller and much fiercer Dytiscus beetle, who liked a meal of stickleback whenever he could get it! The little fish shot backwards like an arrow and managed to get under a stone just in time to save himself from the fierce jaws of the savage beetle. After that he was always careful to make quite certain which beetle it was before he went too close.

In the hot summer days the little stickleback grew very beautiful. He shone with blue and green, and underneath he glowed bright crimson. Then a strange feeling came over him. He longed to make a nest!

'A nest!' said a small frog, when the stickleback told him this. 'What are you thinking of? Are you a bird? Birds make nests. I have seen the moorhen's, and in the hedgerow yonder there are other nests. You are a fish and fish do not make nests.'

'You are wrong,' said the little fish, his three spines standing straight up in annoyance. 'I myself was brought up in a nest. I shall bring my children up in the same way. It is safer. I should not like to do what you frogs do – lay your eggs in a mass and leave them! Why, when the tadpoles hatched out, you should have seen how many were gobbled by the fish, the beetles, and the moorhens! It was terrible to see – though I myself used to like a mouthful of small tadpole, I must say.'

The frog was offended to hear this and swam off in disgust. The stickleback watched him go, and then began to think about his nest again.

'I shall build a beautiful little nest out of weeds and any bits I find floating about the pond,' he thought to himself. 'Then I shall find a pretty stickleback for a wife and make her lay me eggs in my nest. Then I will guard them lovingly until they are hatched.'

Very soon the little creature began to build. He chose a good spot on the bottom of the pond. He swam off to look for any bits floating loose in the water. He was delighted to find many short pieces of grass, pecked up by one of the moorhens and flung into the water. The fish took a piece in his mouth and swam off with it to the place he had chosen. Back he went again and took another piece of grass, and soon he had taken each piece there was and put them all in the spot he had chosen for his nest.

He stuck the pieces carefully together. Then he swam off again to find other bits of hay, straw or leaves. He found what he wanted and swam back to his nest. Carefully he stuck all the bits together and soon a pretty little nest appeared. It was like a muff, with a hole in the middle. The stickleback swam in and out of the muff-like nest in glee, his colours shining brightly. His nest was finished.

'What is this?' asked an ugly creature, rather like an enormous, misshapen earwig, who crawled up to see what the stickleback was doing.

'It's my nest!' said the fish, angrily, darting at the great grub. 'Get away or I will eat you!'

'Eat *me*!' said the grub, scornfully. 'It is much more likely that I shall eat *you*. Look!'

As he spoke he shot out from his face a large pair of horrible-looking pincers, and very nearly snapped off the stickleback's head. The fish backed away just in time.

'You ugly, hideous creature!' cried the fish, angrily. 'Go away!'

'Let me see your nest,' begged the ugly grub. 'I can't help being ugly. I wish I was beautiful, like you, but I never shall be.'

'You can look at my nest, if you like,' said the stickleback. 'But don't be long. I really can't bear the sight of you.'

The grub crawled up to the nest, put his ugly head inside and then crawled away. The stickleback soon forgot him, and began to look for a little wife. He swam all over the pond and at last found one that he liked. He swam up to her and begged her to go to his nest and lay some eggs there.

'No!' said the little stickleback, and swam away. But the fish swam after her angrily and chased her towards his nest. Each time she tried to swim away he darted at her with his spines raised up and she was afraid.

'Go into my beautiful nest and lay me some eggs!' said the stickleback. 'I must have some.'

At last the little fish swam into the nest and laid some eggs there. Then the stickleback let her go, content. He went into the nest to look at his eggs and was disappointed to see that there were only a few. So out he went to look for yet another wife. He soon found one and once more began to chase her to his nest.

She liked the little nest and went into it at once. She laid some eggs there and swam out again. The little stickleback took no further notice of her, but went to see how many eggs there were. Oh, plenty! He was delighted. He went right into the nest and lay there, quite happy.

Presently he saw another stickleback like himself swimming around. The little fish was angry and at once darted out of his nest. He blushed bright red with rage and darted at the other stickleback, trying to tear him with his three sharp spines. The frightened fish swam off at once.

Day after day the little stickleback guarded his nest of eggs. He swam furiously after the ugly water grub who came crawling up again to see the nest. He was so afraid that it might eat his eggs.

'Go away, you ugly creature!' he said. The grub crawled away, sad to hear itself called ugly once again.

The stickleback sometimes stood on his head by the nest and by waving his fins quickly to and fro sent a cool current of water through the nest to aerate his eggs. Once on a very hot day he even spouted water from his mouth into the nest, to make a fresh current for the eggs. He was very proud of his neat little home and cluster of eggs.

At last they hatched out into tiny fish. Then the father stickleback was happier than ever and guarded his nest even more carefully. He knew what tasty morsels those little fish would be to a frog, or grub or the fierce water beetle.

One day the stickleback began to pull the top part of his nest away. The grub came up as he was doing this and watched in surprise.

'Why do you pull your nest to pieces like that?' said the grub.

'I'm not pulling it to pieces,' said the fish. 'My little ones need more room in the nest as they grow. If I pull the top part away they can lie in the bottom half comfortably.

The grub saw the tiny fish lying in the cradle-like nest. There were a great many of them. Their father gazed at them proudly and then looked fiercely round to see if any enemy was near. Ah, that water grub was still there! The fish blazed scarlet and darted at the ugly grub, who at once flashed out its pincers and then crawled hurriedly away.

'Ugly thing!' called the stickleback after it, and then swam back to his nest.

One day the tiny fish were old enough to leave their father's care and go to seek their own fortune. At first they swam about with the big stickleback and he tried to warn them of all the dangers in the pond. He told them of the moorhens who could dive so well, and would snap up a fish easily. He told them of the Dytiscus beetle who would eat a little fish in the flash of a tail. He warned them to beware of the water grub, the ugly fellow who crawled about in the mud.

One by one the tiny fish left their father and went to hunt in the little ditch, or the warm shallows of the pond. At last he was left alone, and he went to look for the ugly grub, to tell him that all his family were now grown. But to his surprise, instead of seeing the grub crawling in the mud, he found him halfway up the stem of a water plant, crawling out into the sunlight.

A still stranger thing happened as he watched. The grub's skin split all the way down his back, and out of the husk came a glorious creature – a great, shining fly with gleaming wings and a long, thin body that shone blue and green in the sunshine!

'You are beautiful!' cried the stickleback,

jumping out of the water to see this marvellous creature better.

'I am a dragonfly!' said the great fly, and spread his gleaming wings out in the sunshine. 'Be careful whom you call ugly in future, stickleback! You never know what they may be going to change into!'

'Come back and tell me about it,' begged the stickleback, excited.

'Never!' cried the dragonfly, and flew off into the sunshine. The stickleback swam off to tell the frogs what had happened – but alas, nobody believed him!